To Kayla

BUMBLE

Happy Reading

FROG

A Chapter Book

By

Suzanne de Board

Suzanne de Board

Also By Suzanne de Board

Pen Pearls – A Personal Anthology

The Gift – Book One in The Gift Series

Merlin's Revenge – Book two in The Gift Series

The Revealing – Book Three in The Gift Series

Sarah Jane

MAYA – Bay of the Dolphin
(A Chapter Book)

Books Coming Soon

The House at Pine-Apple Woods

Lisa

Copyright © 2013 by Suzanne de Board

All rights reserved

ISBN-13 978-1482602838
ISBN-10: 1482602830
Library of Congress Control Number: 2013903549
Create Space, North Charleston, SC

BUMBLE
FROG

BUMBLE FROG

CHAPTER ONE

Bumble Frog stretched in the early morning sun and wriggled his froggy toes in the cool water of his pond home. With his eyes still closed, he smiled a dreamy froggy smile as he dreamt of wonderful things—heroic things, happy things and just plain normal everyday things. Slowly, very slowly, he stretched once more and opened one very bright froggy eye. "Ah, 'tis morning," he croaked, "and all is—"

PLOP   SPLASH

"Hah! Gotcha, Fumble Bumble!"

Bumble swept his tiny froggy hand across his smooth green face wiping droplets of pond water from his very bright froggy eye. Playtime! Pulling his hind feet onto the lily pad, he prepared to leap into the pond and join in the fun, but alas it was not to be, for Bumble Frog soon found himself face first in the water with his hind legs still attached to the lily pad.

Now Bumble's real name was Alexander, but no one ever called him anything cool like Alex or Zander or any other normal name, but Alexander didn't mind. He loved the world and everything in it, and that included the sometimes rude inhabitants of Willow Pond.

Alexander knew he was different, but in his

mind different meant special. He was very different so that *must* mean he was very special, shouldn't it? But the other frogs certainly didn't seem to think so. They made fun of his specialness.

Alexander tried not to take offense when they called him names or refused to play with him, but sometimes it hurt—just a little. But he couldn't really blame them, could he? For you see . . . .

Alexander was his mother's youngest child and he was born . . . well . . . there's no other way to put it. He was *definitely* different. He was smaller than the other frogs his age, but he was blessed with enormous hind legs. So enormous, he put the other frogs to shame. But what good were jumping legs, if there was no one who would play with you? Oh, he tried to play, and everyone had to agree that he could jump higher and farther than *any*one in the pond, but he looked funny, and he had no control.

Day after day he practiced jumping from lily pad to lily pad, but he always overshot his mark, creating huge cannonball splashes or, Heaven help us, landing on some poor innocent's head. No one seemed to care, or understand, how hard he was trying. He was a nuisance, a fumbling, bumbling, nuisance. So he was either ignored or unmercifully teased. But he never gave up. No, he never, ever gave up.

* * *

"Come   on, Peter.   Eat   up," his   mother coaxed. "It will make you grow big and strong."

"Big and strong," Peter muttered as he picked half-heartedly at the breakfast his mother had prepared.

"Peter? As soon as you've cleaned your plate, you can go outside and play. It will do you a world of good."

"Do me good," Peter sighed as he finished his toast, slid sideways in his chair and stared at his feet. "Dumb feet . . . . Dumb leg," he muttered as he slipped off the chair and hobbled to the front door.

"Where will you be, Peter—if I need you, that is?" His mother wiped her hands on her apron as she joined him by the door, planting a quick kiss on the top of his head.

"Thought I'd go by the pond. Check it out . . . . You know."

"Will any of the other boys be going?"

"I don't think so. They've got better things to do with their time . . . I guess. Anyway, I'd rather just go by myself."

Peter's slight limp seemed somewhat exaggerated as he made his way down the pathway and into the nearby woods. Concern filled his mother's eyes as she watched him go. *He needs a friend*, she sighed. *Someone who will understand . . . . Understand and care about a little lost boy.*

CHAPTER TWO

Peter scrunched down behind some bayberry bushes near the big old willow tree and watched with interest the antics going on at Willow Pond. *That frog needs help*, he thought, as Alexander tried unsuccessfully 'just one more time' to land on a particular lily pad. "Come on, frog," he whispered. "You can do it." But Peter was mistaken.

It wasn't from lack of trying, Peter gave him that, but maybe he was just trying too hard. "Ease off a bit," he whispered once more, but Alexander was too intent on landing on the huge lily pad, in the center of the pond, to pay attention, even if he

8 Suzanne de Board

would have been able to hear Peter's whispered words of encouragement.

After several minutes of unsuccessful attempts, Alexander was about to give up when something deep inside him said, "You can do it. Just one last try, and then you can quit." So, stretching his enormous legs, he took an enormous leap. But instead of landing on the lily pad, he missed the pond completely, landing on a drooping willow branch high above the mud bank at the edge of the pond.

"Hah! Fumble Bumble!" jeered the other frogs as he struggled to hang onto the slippery bough with his tiny froggy fingers. But his enormous hind legs were just too heavy, and he fell into the soft mud beneath him.

"Oof," he gasped as he hit the ground, the breath knocked quite out of him. He kept his eyes tightly shut as he lay on his back gasping for what little breath he had left.

"Are you all right?"

Alexander opened his right eye and then his left staring blurrily at the little boy kneeling in front of him.

"A boy! It's a human boy! Hide!" he heard amidst the plops and splashes of the other frogs disappearing beneath the surface of the pond. Alexander panicked, tried to right himself and escape, but found he couldn't move.

For the first time in his young life, Alexander

hated his enormous hind legs. They were just too heavy, and trying to escape was useless. His tiny fingers and his oversized toes ceased twitching as he collapsed, closing his eyes, waiting . . . waiting . . . to die.

"Poor old frog," said the boy as he reached out, gently lifting him from the mud with one hand while scooping water from the pond with his other hand, rinsing the mud from Alexander's back and legs. "Are you all right?"

Alexander opened first his right eye, then his left, and stared into the deepest blue eyes he had ever seen. He was alive! The human boy had not killed him and seemed to be trying to help, *but* he was still a boy and Alexander didn't want to take any chances. His tiny limp body became springy once again as he tried desperately to escape the boy's grasp.

"Whoa," laughed the boy. "You *are* all right. Don't worry. I'm not going to hurt you." Peter carefully sat the little frog near the edge of the pond and watched as he leapt into the water, swam quickly to the center of the pond, and hid behind a giant-sized lily pad floating there.

Tiny froggy eyes peered at the boy as he stood by the water's edge watching Alexander with great interest. Finally the boy turned to leave.

"Good-bye, frog," called the little boy, almost forgetting his bad leg as he reluctantly began to limp toward home, his hands in his pockets, whistling a merry little tune.

Alexander watched the boy until he disappeared from sight, a mixture of curiosity and . . . and . . . he wasn't sure what, filling his mind and heart. *Oh well*, he sighed as he climbed onto the lily pad. *Perhaps he'll come again . . . and then we will see what we will see.*

He yawned as big a yawn as he could muster, and promptly fell asleep.

CHAPTER THREE

"Peter . . . ? Peter! Where are you going? You've hardly touched your breakfast."

Peter limped back to the kitchen table as fast as his lame leg would let him, gulped down the rest of his orange juice, and grabbed a piece of toast before heading back to the front door. "Sorry, Mama. I guess I'm just not hungry . . . much. But I have my lunch. See?"

"Stop right there, young man. I want to see what's in that bag."

"But, Mom," Peter hedged, slipping the paper bag behind his back.

"No buts. You've disappeared everyday this week, and I want to know what's going on." She softened just a bit before adding, "I worry about you, -Peter. You spend so much time alone. You don't have any friends—"

"But the kids around here . . . ."

"Yes?"

"Aw, nothin'. Can I go now? I gotta be somewhere."

"After I see what's in the bag." Resting one hand on his shoulder, she sighed and held out her free hand. "The bag, Peter."

Reluctantly Peter handed his mother his lunch bag before slipping his hand into his jeans pocket, his index finger nervously playing with the thinning material until he poked a small hole in the lining.

"Hmmm. It looks . . . alright . . . . Ugh! What's this? Worms? Grasshoppers? Some lunch this is. Oh," she flashed a hopeful smile. "Are we planning on going fishing with a friend?"

"Nope. Goin' froggin'."

"Frogging? Well . . . I guess I could cook up a mess of legs . . . if you can catch enough. Here." She handed the bag back to Peter with a thoughtful expression on her face. "Happy hunting." She shut the door behind him, and as the latch slipped into place, muttered, "Frog legs? Hmmm. How in the world do you cook frog legs?"

Peter knew his mother would be disappointed, but there was no way he was going to cook his new little frog friend, or any other frog for that matter.

Frogs were smart. Frogs were funny, and frogs were

friendly . . . once you got to know them.

CHAPTER FOUR

Peter peered cautiously around the old willow tree, spreading the branches apart just a bit, watching the rippling of the water as the tips of the branches popped in and out of the pond.

"Psst. Hey, Frog," he whispered loudly. "Frog! I've got something for ya. Where are ya, Frog?"

Alexander opened one sleepy eye and stretched a mighty stretch before skimming across the pond toward the boy's voice. He'd never had a boy before, and he had been told human boys were bad news and to stay away from them. But this boy was different.

This boy was smart, and funny, and friendly; not at all like the other boys who occasionally came to the pond for a swim, or to torture the pond dwellers. And he had a nice name . . . Peter. With only his very bright froggy eyes showing above the surface of the water, Alexander searched the shoreline of the pond. "Where are you, boy?" he croaked just before Peter popped into view.

"Here I am, Frog. Are you ready for another lesson? I've brought lunch." He held up the paper bag.

Alexander hopped up to Peter and stared at the brown paper bag. *Yum.* His tongue flicked out for a treat, and he frowned at the taste of the paper.

Peter pulled the bag away and laughed. "Whoa,

Frog. Gotta learn to jump *right* first, then we eat."

Alexander frowned once again and sighed a tiny froggy sigh before turning to his left and hopping along the rim of the pond to the thick green willow curtain hugging the ground before him.

To the average eye, this curtain was the end of the trail. You could go no further. But to the frog and his boy, another world waited just beyond. "Come on, Boy," he croaked, his tiny stomach rumbling. "Let's get on with this, so we can eat."

Peter, not understanding frog talk, hurried along as fast as his lame leg would let him, just as anxious, in his own way, to enter the tunnel and cross over into the beauty of the hidden meadow. Reaching the thick willow curtain, he dropped to his knees, thrust his arm through the middle and spread the branches apart. "You first, Frog," he whispered.

Excitement began to fill Alexander's tiny body as he hopped though the opening and into the tangled tunnel of grasses and weeds in front of him. Only a small animal, or a boy willing enough to make the journey and squeeze through the tight fit, would ever have attempted such a feat. But Peter was brave, and Peter was determined, *and* Peter now knew what lay on the other side.

The tunnel wasn't long, but it took a bit longer for Peter to crawl through than Alexander. Being a human boy, of course, made a big difference, but Peter was also stopping every foot or so, and pushing his body tightly against the top and sides of the tunnel. Every time he went into the tunnel he pushed and stretched and pushed again, forcing the tunnel to become a little bit larger to better accommodate a boy his size.

If he sucked in his stomach, he could make it through without touching . . . almost. The first time he went through, he had had to slide through *on* his stomach, but now? Piece-of-cake . . . almost.

He grinned at the not-so-patient Alexander, as his head and shoulders slipped out of the tunnel and into the meadow. *Wow.* He sat on his haunches and stared at the meadow. *This is so cool.* At one time, long ago, someone had obviously been there.

A large uneven patch of ground had been cleared, surrounded by very tall reeds and sprinkled with colorful bamboo, lining a pathway at the far end of the clearing to . . . who knows where. Bamboo was not native to these parts so Peter knew that someone had to have planted it, but when, and why?

Patches of wildflowers, and flowering plants Peter had seen only in the nurseries his mother had taken him to before they had had to move, bloomed everywhere.

Alexander croaked once again, bringing Peter back to the present. "Okay, Frog, I'm comin'." Peter struggled to stand, grabbing a stout stick he had left there just for this very purpose.

Being extra careful not to trample the ground cover, the two stepped, and/or hopped, cautiously over to the obstacle course set out for Alexander's training. Smooth, flat stones, some large, some small, set out at various distances from each other, beckoned the trainer and the trainee. The beauty of the meadow temporarily forgotten, the two began in earnest to train, train, train.

"You've almost got it, Frog," Peter shouted encouragement, as Alexander's left big toe grazed the far edge of the largest of the stones. "Try it again, but this time don't flex quite so hard. You can do it. I know you can . . . . Aw . . . that's all right, Frog. You've worked really hard. We'll try again tomorrow, okay?"

Alexander nodded. He felt really good about himself. That last jump was closest yet, and he had only been training for three days. Just wait. Soon he would be able to join the other frogs, and they would *have* to play with him, then. No more Fumble Bumble. At last, he knew that someday he *would* fit in.

He jumped high into the air, did a backwards flip, and landed on his enormous hind legs. As his tiny front feet touched the ground, no one seemed to notice that he had landed in the very spot from which he had taken off. Hmmmm.

With his tiny shoulders squared, as much as a young frog can, he hopped to the nearby pathway leading to who-knows-where and waited for Peter to join him. Next to his training sessions, this was the most fun part of the day. The pathway was wide and straight, and perfect for racing. And that is what they did.

At the end of every day, Peter would draw a new line in the dirt at the beginning of the pathway and count one—two—three, and they were off. They only raced as long as the path was straight, before turning and racing back.

It seemed safe enough . . . as long as the path was straight, but when it turned hard to the right, narrowed and disappeared into the darkness of the forest . . . well, it seemed the better part of valor to stay where they were and not to take any unnecessary chances.

Alexander stood at the finish line and waited. He always won. He croaked a happy chorus, encouraging Peter as he half hobbled, half ran, back up the raceway. *You can do it*, he seemed to say, and Peter grinned as he pushed himself just a little bit harder to cross the finish line. He felt good. He felt proud of himself. He never won, but that was to be expected.

Every day he got just a little bit closer to the finish line before having to stop and walk the rest of the way. Just ten more feet and he would make it. Nine . . . eight . . . almost . . . .

But almost didn't quite make it as his feet slowed and he began to hobble once again. Huffing and puffing he crossed the finish line, elated that he had made it as far as he had before his lame leg had given out. "Well, Frog. How'd I do?"

In answer, Alexander hopped to the brown paper

bag and flicked out his tongue. It was time to eat . . .

for a job well done.

CHAPTER FIVE

"Coming, Peter? Please try and hurry. We're going to be late."

"Aw, Ma. Do I hafta go? I've got plans . . . things to do."

"Come on, Peter. Don't dawdle. Yes, you have to come. I've barely seen you for more than three weeks now. I want to spend some time with you. After all, I *am* your mother. We'll stop and get ice cream after the shopping is done. Wouldn't you like that? And, you might find some new friends in town."

Ice cream sounded great, and spending time

with his mom didn't sound too bad either. She was

lonely, too. He knew that, and he felt bad for her,

but they were making so much progress, he and

Frog. He didn't need new friends, and they didn't

need him. He sighed. Frog had turned out to be his

best friend . . . his only friend, next to his mother,

that is.

But mothers *have* to be your friend, it's the law,

he knew. But special friends were few and far

between, and a frog friend . . . well, that was the

best.

They had worked hard, and Frog was getting

down this jumping thing pretty well. He could make

two out of three jumps most of the time, and even

though he wasn't perfect, he tried really hard,

and then   there were   the races . . . and—

"Peter! Are you coming? I'm leaving . . . . I'm
in the car . . . . I'm starting the engine . . . ."

Peter glanced around the living room, sighed
and shut the door, securing the lock before hobbling
toward his waiting mom. What else could he do?
But what about Frog? He was expecting him. He
would be so disappointed. He couldn't even practice
without someone lifting aside the willow branches.

He slid into the passenger seat and slammed
the door, quickly fastening his seat belt. Staring
mournfully out of his side window, he watched the
woods recede as his mother drove slowly down the
washboard road leading to the two-lane highway and
town.

"Sorry, Frog," he mumbled, closing his eyes, wishing he was at the pond instead of on his way into town. "Don't miss me too bad. I'll see ya tomorrow, just see if I won't."

* * *

Alexander waited . . . and waited . . . and waited. Something was wrong. Something was wrong with his boy. Was he hurt? Was he sick? Why didn't he come? It was late. He should have been here hours ago.

With his tiny froggy shoulders slumped, he hopped slowly to the water's edge and slid in. Gliding to the far side of the pond, he chose a lily pad to rest his front feet and head on, allowing the rest of his body to float aimlessly in the water.

Alexander was worried. Alexander was lonely. But all he could do was wait . . . wait for a boy who may never come. "Boy," he croaked sadly. "Where are you?" And closed his tiny eyes.

CHAPTER SIX

Peter yawned, slid back his covers and stretched, as he threw his legs over the side of his bed and sat up. Another day of drudgery, he sighed. Frog must be worried. It had been almost a week since he'd been to the pond, and he hoped that Frog was all right.

For some crazy reason his mother had chosen this week to practice her canning. And Peter, of course, was expected to help. It was still six weeks until the County Fair. She had plenty of time to practice. Why now?

He slid his feet into his over-sized leather slippers, slipped on his robe and ambled into the kitchen. The smell of breakfast was overwhelming, and he was starving.

"Good morning, Peter. Have a good sleep?"

"It was all right, I guess. What're we doin' today?"

"Well, I thought, now that the canning is done, I would just putter around the house a bit, do some mending, you know, all of that sort of thing, and I thought maybe I could put you to work . . . just kidding. As of today, you are a free man, within reason of course. Anything particular you'd like to do today? Hmmmm?" she grinned.

"Do ya mean it, Ma? Can I go out to the pond, or . . . or . . . well, can I?"

"As soon as you finish your breakfast. I know

whomever, or whatever, is out there must have missed you a great deal. But it was nice having your attention for a little while at least." She smiled indulgently.

"Gee, shanks, Ma." Peter wolfed down his breakfast as his mother reminded him to *'not talk with your mouth full.'*

"I can't understand a word you're saying," she scolded with obvious affection. "Slow down a bit. You'll choke." But minutes his breakfast was gone, he was dressed, and out the door.

"Wait a minute, young man," his mother called from the open doorway. "Didn't you forget something?" She held a brown paper bag at arm's length, but when Peter reached for it, quickly hid it behind her back, extending her right cheek for a kiss good-bye.

"Aw, Ma," he blushed, giving her a quick peck on the cheek.

"I love you, Peter," she smiled, handing him the paper bag surprise.

"You too, Ma," Peter replied. With one last hug, he turned and raced toward the pond. He could hardly wait. "Hope Frog hasn't forgotten all about me," he muttered to himself. *Yippee!*

* * *

Alexander tried, he really tried, but he couldn't quite seem to get in the spirit, without his boy. He was too small to squeeze through the willow curtain to the practice field, and even though he tried to jump onto imaginary stones along the perimeter of the pond, he just wasn't very successful. The jeers of the other s didn't help, and the name Fumble Bumble continuously ran through his head.

Of course, it wouldn't have been so bad if he didn't hear the name constantly thrown at him from his fellow frogs. He had to admit, it still hurt to be called names and to be made fun of. But where was the boy . . . his boy?

Peter would never laugh at him, would never call him names. But Peter was not here. Perhaps he would never come again. Alexander sighed a small froggy sigh and buried himself halfway into the mud under the giant willow. *Boy . . . where are you*?

Alexander fell asleep, a tiny tear escaping from

one tiny froggy eye.

* * *

"Hey, Frog!" Peter whispered loudly—loud enough, he hoped, for Alexander to hear, but not enough to startle the other frogs.

By now the other pond inhabitants were used to the 'human boy' and were prone to ignore him. After all, he never seemed to bother anyone, and besides, if he was a friend of Fumble Bumble, well, two of a kind they were and not to be taken seriously by anyone.

So they left the boy and Bumble alone. They weren't 'play with' material anyway, so what did it matter? As long as the two didn't bother them, they couldn't care less what they did or didn't do for that matter.

Humph, they croaked, whenever Peter came to visit, then turned their backs and paid them no attention whatsoever. This was just fine for Alexander. It helped him keep his secret just a little bit better, for a little bit longer.

"Hi, Frog." Peter stroked Alexander's smooth head, gently, just enough to awaken him but not enough to scare him into disappearing back into the pond. "I'm back," he whispered. "Did ya miss me?"

Alexander's tiny eyes flew open, staring for just a moment at his best friend, before shaking off the mud and leaping into Peter's arms.

"Hey, Frog," Peter laughed, "you got me all muddy. What'd ya do that for?" But Alexander knew that Peter didn't really mind the mud and was just as happy to see him as Alexander was to see Peter.

"Sorry I'm late. I hope you weren't too worried about me. My mother needed my help real bad. I don't know why she had to pick now to practice her canning, but it's done now, so are you ready to go practice some jumpin'?"

Alexander leapt from Peter's arms into the pond, and swam a quick lap around the perimeter before hopping back onto the bank. By now Peter had dusted the mud off of his shirt and was waiting by the willow curtain for Alexander's return.

The fumbling, bumbling little frog was so excited to see Peter, and to know he had not been forgotten, he hopped so high and so far, he landed on the slippery willow curtain instead of the ground in front of the mossy green tunnel.

Peter reached out and grabbed him just before he hit the ground, lowering him gently to the tunnel entrance before spreading the curtain apart and ushering Alexander through. "You'd better be more careful," he warned with a chuckle. "You could have been hurt. You're lucky I was here to catch you."

Alexander rubbed his tiny head against Peter's leg, as if to say thank you, before hopping through the tunnel and onto the training field. Peter lost no time in following, this time not stopping to enlarge the tunnel.

It was just big enough for a small boy to slip through comfortably, and not have to slide through. *Wow! What a difference a week made.* The wild irises were blooming, and the yellow and white daisies surrounding them were . . . well, he knew that when it was time to leave he just had to take a bouquet home to his mother. After all, they didn't belong to anybody, and they would make his mother so happy.

If anything, they belonged to Frog and himself. They discovered them so they had rights, didn't they? Alexander began to croak, calling Peter back to the task at hand. Peter stood and carefully made his way to the now familiar training course. "Okay, Frog," he commanded. "Let's see what you can do."

The pair was so intent on their training, they failed to notice two dark eyes, curious eyes, blinking in the shadows of the reeds, inches from the ground, just waiting and watching, watching and waiting for what was to come.

CHAPTER SEVEN

Alexander's mind raced as his tiny body flew down the makeshift track. He grinned a big froggy grin as he turned his head just enough to catch a glimpse of Peter, but not far enough to lose his balance and trip up. His boy was remarkable.

Peter didn't realize just how far he had come over the past few weeks. He hardly ever limped anymore, and he was getting faster with every race. He knew Peter thought that he, Alexander, was slowing down just to make him look good, but Peter still tried all the harder, ran all the faster, hoping, just hoping that some day he might win.

The funny thing was, Alexander was trying his best, but Peter was gaining strength every time they raced. Alexander was beginning to think that Peter actually would win—someday.

But not today, he grinned once more. *Not today.* He sprinted toward the finish line. He stretched his tiny neck as far as it would go. His hops became longer . . . higher . . . . Almost there.

SWOOSH

Alexander was gone.

"Wha . . . ?" Peter stumbled, his arms spinning like a windmill, attempting to catch himself before falling head first onto the hard packed path. "Frog!" he shouted. "Where are you?" He slid to a stop, looking more like a baseball player sliding into home plate, than a track star.

CRASH!

Peter scrambled to his feet and stood face to face with the frog-napper. He was a boy, about eleven years old, and at least a head taller than Peter. He was barefoot and wore tattered khaki shorts with a torn dirty tank top. Peter stared at the intruder but he felt no fear. "Give me back my frog," he demanded.

"Your what?" he snickered. "You mean this scrawny little critter with the oversized hind legs. This itty, bitty no good critter." He held Alexander in his right hand as high as he could reach above his head. "Shorley not. This critter is mine. I caught him fair and square. My grandpap shore does love legs cooked up crispy like, and there's a whole lot of leg here, wouldn't ya say?"

Peter grabbed for his best friend, but the boy was just too tall, and much too quick as he danced about, bringing Alexander just within Peter's reach before thrusting him high into the air again, whooping and laughing at Peter's feeble, though heroic, attempts to free the tiny frog. With a sudden burst of adrenaline Peter's fist shot out making contact with the stranger's nose.

"Hey, what'd ya do that for?" The boy rubbed his sore nose and glared at Peter.

"Give—me—back—my—frog," he growled, his fists balled at his sides, while Alexander hung limp and terrified, from the stranger's hand.

"Cain't. He belongs t' me. He used t' belong to you but now he belongs t' me, and I have a hankerin' for some frog legs real bad."

Alexander began to struggle as Peter swung once again. But this time the boy was ready and dodged the intended blow. Time and again Peter swung on this new foe, and time and again the boy danced just out of reach, laughing at Peter's frustration.

"Hey, kid. You wanna know why he's mine now, and not yours? 'Cause you stole my grandpap's flowers, so I get your frog. Fair is fair, you know."

Peter stopped swinging, and with his hands on his knees puffed, "What are you talking 'bout. I didn't steal anything."

"You shore did. This here meadow belongs to me and grandpap and you stole our flowers. So this here frog is mine. Yummm."

"Those flowers belonged to you? But I didn't know. They were just there, growing wild, so I picked some for my mom." He paused, his eyes narrowing to near slits. "How do I know the meadow's yours?" Peter asked suspiciously, his fists once again tightly balled. "My mom says the meadow doesn't belong to anyone. Anybody can come here."

"If they can find their way in, I suppose. But even if that's true, my grandpap planted those bulbs and stuff before I was ever born. You don't see *those* kind of flowers growin' wild. They're special, and you stole 'em so I get the frog."

"You can't eat Frog. *He's* special. I've been training him. He's—" Peter's eyes began to mist and he was trying hard not to cry.

"Oh, brother. Here, take your old fog. I was just kiddin', anyways. Just funnin' with ya.   I wouldn't have eaten him. I like frogs—fresh or cooked. Just kiddin'."

He raised his left hand to protect his sore nose, grinning as he dropped Alexander into Peter's waiting arms. He held out his right hand and said, "Friends? Gordy's the name. Actually, it's Gordon, like my grandpap, but everybody calls me Gordy."

Peter wasn't sure whether he wanted to forgive

this strange kid or not, but finally stretched out his own hand, reluctantly shaking the hand of his former antagonist.

"Peter," he mumbled, and then clearing his throat repeated, "Peter. My name's Peter—and this is Frog."

"Glad to meet ya, Pete. What are ya gonna do with uh . . . Frog? Gonna enter him in the big race?"

"Race? What race?"

"Where've ya been, Pete? The annual Labor Day Picnic and County Fair. There's all kinds of contests, and best of all, the frog jumpin' races.

"Of course the kids race too, but it's nothin' like the frog race. Jeremy Jacobs wins every year, but with Frog here, I'll bet he'll leave Germy Jeremy's frog in the dust. How 'bout it? Wanta give it a try? It'll take a lot more trainin', but I could help . . . if you want me to, that is. My grandpap gave me a stop watch. We could time him and—"

"I don't know . . . . It's up to Frog. When is this race anyway?"

"Three weeks from Monday, on the fifth of September. You'll have to work really hard if you're gonna beat Germy Jeremy. What d'ya say? Huh? What d'ya say?"

"Well . . . I don't know. What do you think, Frog? Do you wanna race?"

In answer, Alexander sprang from Peter's arms, hopped to the end of the pathway, and assumed the racer's pose, shifting from foot to foot, head down, streamlined and ready to go.

"Okay," laughed Peter. "Go get your watch. We've got practicin' to do."

CHAPTER EIGHT

The next two weeks passed quickly, filled with training, racing, and camaraderie. Gordy showed up, as regular as clockwork, with his grandfather's stop watch, eager to see just how fast Alexander was becoming and just as eager to see him topple the king, Germy Jeremy.

It had long been suspected that Jeremy was a cheater, but since it could not be proven, there was nothing to do but try their best and hope to win. With only one week and two days to go 'til the big race, Peter and Gordy were full of last minute advice.

Alexander listened carefully and tried to do as he was instructed, but he was, after all, a frog, and frogs like to do what they do best—hop like the wind.

Yesterday, Gordy's grandpap had stopped by, and after careful observation pronounced Alexander ready to go, with an "excellent chance of beatin' the competition—all the competition, if somebody doesn't cheat, that is," he had said, stroking his chin. "Yes, an excellent chance."

Peter grinned at his new best friend . . . after Frog, of course. Yes, Alexander was as ready as he would ever be, but they couldn't rest now. It wouldn't do to take even one day for play, with so much at stake.

YAHOO   GET 'EM

OVER HERE   THAT ONE

Peter stared at Gordy as he lifted his finger to his lips. "Shhhh." Where was all that screaming, shouting and laughter coming from? Splashing . . . screaming . . . . Whoever it was must be terrifying the poor creatures in the pond.

As silently as he could, Peter ran to the reed tunnel and crawled through to the other side, stopping just short of the willow curtain.

Alexander cringed. He knew what it was, and so did Gordy, but Peter . . . ? *He* would soon find out. Alexander slowly wriggled his way past Peter and rested under his chest, watching. Just watching and waiting.

"Got one," shouted the little boy with the oversized straw hat.

"Me, too," hollered another triumphantly.

Peter and Alexander watched as one by one the pond frogs were captured and stuffed into small boxes, or bags tied securely to a belt loop on each boy's best froggin' jeans. *Oh, no,* thought Peter. *They're scaring them to death. That's no way to catch a frog.* But catch them they did, one after the other until there were no more to be seen or heard.

* * *

Only one boy, tall and thin, with slicked-back blond hair, stood alone, leaning back against the old willow, his arms crossed, watching this traditional 'Gathering of the frogs.' All the frogs were gone, at least all the good ones, but he wasn't worried. He was confident that he would win . . . one way or the other. After all, he always did.

He grinned to himself. These frogs were nothin'. His frog was a champion. No one else stood even half a chance, so he was content. Granted, he didn't have his frog yet, but he would. His dad had promised, like he did every year, and he was confident he would come through.

"Losers," he muttered. "Losers, every one of 'em."

* * *

Alexander crawled inside Peter's t-shirt, struggling toward the rounded neck and stuck his head out, just under Peter's chin.

"Hold still, Frog," Peter whispered to the quaking little frog, gently patting the lump under his shirt. "*You* are the best. Don't worry about them. It's them who don't have a chance, not you. Okay?"

Alexander quieted down and the pair watched as the boys from town left the pond, still full of high spirits and confidence in their own individual frog.

* * *

The boy with the slicked-back blond hair brought up the rear, a few paces behind, stopping once to gaze back at the pond and shake his head. *Nothin' great has ever come out of this pond, and nothin' ever will. It's in the bag.*

He grinned to himself, and holding his head high, strutted after the masses. It is *so* in the bag.

CHAPTER NINE

"Come on, Mom. We're going to be late. We've gotta hurry."

"I'm coming, I'm coming." Peter's mother looked at her only son and sighed a happy sigh. What a difference a summer made. No longer withdrawn, he had become a different person.

His new friend must have been really special to produce such a difference. She had yet to meet him, or her, and was hoping that this would be the day. But if he made Peter happy, she was happy. And Peter was definitely happy.

She gathered the last of her entries and placed

them in the trunk of her car. She hadn't intended to enter so many items, but once she got started, well . . . you know how it is. She grinned at Peter as she slipped into the driver's side and started the engine. "Are you ready?" she quizzed, already well aware of the answer.

"Past, Mom." Peter's excitement was contagious as he bounced beneath the seatbelt securely fastening him to the passenger seat of their only transportation. Fifteen minutes later, they had parked and Peter was standing beside his opened car door. *Wow*. Peter had never been to a county fair, and he stood in awe at the sights, sounds and smells.

"Peter . . . . Peter? Mom to Peter . . . . Mom to

Peter." She grinned at the wonder in Peter's eyes . . . on his face. "Peter. I'm going to need your help in getting all these entries in place, so don't run off."

"Okay, Mom." He patted his shirt pocket and whispered, "You okay, Frog?"

Alexander poked his head out of the oversized pocket and flicked out his tongue, planting a sticky, froggy kiss on Peter's neck. Peter began to giggle as his mother came around the corner of the vehicle.

"Oh, Peter," she smiled. "You've caught yourself a little frog. How cute." She reached out to gently rub his tiny head with her empty hand, before transferring the crafts from her other arm into Peter's waiting hands. "Here, sweetheart," she said. "Carry these for me, will you?"

"Sure, Mom," Peter answered, as his mother turned, and lifting the first of many boxes, started for the tent marked 'Home Arts.' It seemed like forever, but at last the car was unpacked, his mother was filling out the entry forms, and he was free to do whatever he wanted to do.

He picked up a flyer and searched for the time and place for the races. "Two o'clock. That's hours from now," he mumbled to himself. Just to be on the safe side, he had better find where the races were going to be held. He didn't want to be late. Frog deserved to have his chance and Peter was going to see that he got it.

"Pssst. Pete. Hey. . . *Pe-ter*." Peter turned and saw Gordy peeking out from behind some barrels near the make-shift stables. "Come 'ere, I wanta show ya somethin'."

Peter sprinted toward the stables, and as he reached Gordy he was pulled roughly behind the flap of the tent. Leaning tightly against the canvas wall, Gordy whispered, "We're not supposed to be in here, but I wanted to show ya something'."

With Peter close to his side, Gordy skirted the stalls until he reached the one at the very end of the tent, partially hidden from prying eyes. "Look. Ain't he somethin'?"

Peter stared at the newborn foal, his eyes huge with wonder. "Wow," he gulped. "What is it?"

"It's a colt, a baby horse. Haven't you ever seen one before?"

"No, I—"

Gordy yanked on Peter's shirt, pulling him to the ground. "Shhhh. Someone's comin'," he whispered a warning.

The boys lay as quietly as possible in the hay next to the stall, as Gordy proceeded to cover them with straw strewn about the floor. "Shhhh."

A tall man entered from the back of the tent, carefully glancing about before motioning for someone to join him. "It's the kid from the pond," Peter whispered.

"That's not just any kid," Gordy whispered back. "That's Germy Jeremy and his pa."

Peter knew that it wasn't polite to listen in on someone else's conversation, but what could they do? They were trapped, and so they became privy to information that no one else knew, but most suspected.

"Now, son. I cannot stress enough just how important it is for you to win this race. If I am going to win my bid for Mayor, I need to have a winning family. I will accept nothing less. Do you understand, Son."

"I'm with you, Pop."

"Don't call me Pop, at least in public. It's so common, and we Jacobs are never common. That's why becoming the Mayor would . . . well, never mind. The object is that Jacobs never lose, they always win, what*ever* it takes. I expect you to follow in my footsteps, boy.

"Now don't disappoint me. You know how I get when I'm disappointed, don't you, Son? I need a family beside me who are winners in every way. So get out and win, win, win." He patted the boy and smiled a smile as slick as the hair on his only son's head.

"Uh . . . Dad? What am I supposed to win with?"

"What? Oh, silly me. I almost forgot. I have the best frog money can buy. He has never lost a race. He is a champion of champions. No one, not one, has a chance against him. He—"

"But, Dad. When do I get him?"

"All in good time, son. All in good time. I cannot stress how important it is to win this race. If you lose, which you cannot possibly do, but on the off chance that you do, do not bother to come home.

"Only winners are in our family, and I will be hard pressed to believe you are my son if you are not a winner. Understand, Son?"

"Sure, Dad. Don't worry. I've seen all the other frogs. They're nothin', nothin' at all."

"Wonderful. Then we won't have a problem . . . will we, Son . . . ? I thought not."

The boys breathed a sigh of relief when the pair finally left the stables. "He cheated," exclaimed Peter. "How can he get away with that?"

"Like I said, everybody always suspected, but nobody could ever prove nothin'. Now we got the proof. But let's not tell anybody just yet."

"Why not?"

"'Cause they don't know it, but they're gonna lose— big time."

CHAPTER TEN

Peter grimaced, holding his ears with both hands as the shrill squawk of the out-of-date microphone jangled the nerves of contestants and spectators alike.

Tap   Tap   Tap   SQUEEEAL

Tap   Tap   Tap

"LADIES AND GENTLEMEN," bellowed the announcer. "Uh . . . sorry about that.   Technical difficulties, you know. Anyway . . . . Let's try that again.

"Ladies, gentlemen, contestants, and those just hangin' around for a good time . . . what you've all been waitin' for . . . *the* fantastic, *world* famous, (at least in our part of the world) *fabulous* frog jumpin', frog racin' contest. We have contestants from all over the valley, and we—"

Peter stretched and strained, searching with his eyes for his mom. *Ma, where are you? The contest is about to start. Where are you, Ma?* He stood alone, pacing in place, excited, but nervous at the same time.

His mother had not yet returned from the 'Home Arts' tent and he had yet to find out how she had fared in all the contests. But this was so important. This was Frog's big chance . . . his special day . . . a day to prove himself as the best of the best.

It wouldn't be the same if his mom wasn't there

when they won the big trophy sitting on the card table right next to the announcer. What a beauty. He wondered if Gordy could see it from wherever he was.

* * *

While Peter was waiting for his chance with Frog, Gordy was out looking for Germy Jeremy and his father. Cheaters. He didn't want to get caught, of course, but he sure would like to be there when 'the germ' received the illegal champion frog.

How he would love to turn them in, now, before the contest even started, but even more he wanted to see Frog whip the crispy fried legs off o' that frog and his cheating owners. The rules were clear. All frogs must be local frogs. No imported or out of state. County frogs, fine. But nothing else. "Whoa . . . ."

There they were—Jeremy, his dad, and the biggest frog Gordy had ever seen. His legs were as big as Frog's and he was six times the size. Anybody could tell he wasn't a local, but Mr. Jacobs was a powerful man, and would probably lie about it and convince the judges that . . . . Gordy began to feel sick.

He should tell Pete, but how could he do that to his best friend . . . his only friend . . . besides grandpap, that is. He watched as the monster champion frog was put back in the box, and the duo strolled confidently toward the starting gate. *Better get back to Pete. He's gotta know about this.*

Cheaters. Cheaters. Cheaters.

* * *

Peter was getting antsy, no Mom and no Gordy.

Where is everybody? There he is. Peter flashed

Gordy a big grin as he loomed into sight, but his

smile quickly faded at the look on Gordy's face.

"What's the matter?" he asked as Gordy finally

reached him.

"You don't wanta know," he replied with a

whisper. "What's goin' on?"

"Oh. They're doing things different this year.

Since there's so many entries, they're going to

divide up all the owners into age groups—kids

eleven and under, and kids twelve and up. Then the

winners of the age groups race, and then the winner

of that race wins the trophy."

"ATTENTION . . . . ATTENTION, PLEASE."
The announcer boomed. "ALL CONTESTANTS
ELEVEN AND UNDER . . . . TO THE STARTING
LINE."

"Hey! That's us. Gotta go. Wish us luck."

"Not so fast, young man." Peter's mother
seemed to have appeared from out of nowhere as she
bent and gave him a quick kiss on the top of his
head. "For luck," she smiled.

"Thanks, Mom." A quick hug and he was gone.
When he saw the other boys with their freshly
caught pond frogs, he couldn't help but grin. *Frog is
so much better, so much stronger, so much . . . .*

"Okay, boys. What I need is for you lads to keep your frogs corralled by someone you trust, while you run on down to the finish line and cheer your frog to victory. First frog to cross the line, finish line, that is, wins. Okay boys, who's it gonna be?"

Before Peter could turn around and look, Gordy was at his side, lifting Alexander gently from his hands. "Piece o' cake," he whispered with a grin. "I got it from this side."

* * *

Alexander's confidence began to fade, just a bit, when he heard the croaking jeers and taunts of the other frogs at the starting line. He sighed as the ones he used to call his friends turned their backs on him, their tiny snooty noses in the air. Could he beat them? Was he good enough, or was he really a failure as they said? His tiny head drooped, and he sighed once more.

* * *

Peter gently ran his hand down Alexander's back, and said, "Don't forget, Frog. You're the best of the best. Don't let these guys scare you. They're just a bunch of pussy willows."

"Come on now, boys. Let's hurry it up. We haven't got all day, you know."

Peter, hobbling to the finish line, suddenly remembered his lame leg, and all the people who were watching. He sank down onto his haunches and called out, "You can do it, Frog. All ya have to do is try your best."

"Ready . . . set . . . . Boys . . . call your frogs."

What a madhouse. Frogs were everywhere. Only a few hopped in the right direction, others tried to escape toward what they thought to be the way to the pond, and still others refused to jump at all. Boys were screaming. Boys were chasing. *And* boys were pushing their frogs toward the finish line. But where was Alexander?

Peter stood, held Alexander over his head, and beamed.

"WE HAVE A WINNER," bellowed the announcer. "Fastest frog I've ever seen. Seemed to know just what he was doin'. That's some frog, son. Congratulations."

The losing frogs were finally gathered by their

temporary owners and placed back in their containers, ready to be loosed back into the pond as soon as the final race was over. The boys didn't seem to mind losing and looked at Peter with an admiration they had not shown before.

Peter was elated. Peter was flying high. Frog had done just what he had set out to do. He cradled him close to his chest and told him over and over again how wonderful he was. *Now, if the older boys' frogs were as . . . oh, no.*

Peter watched in shock, his stomach plummeting into his shoes, as Jeremy Jacobs lifted his monster frog from the cardboard box, specially prepared for such a champion. He listened as the quiet grumble of the crowd swept through the perimeter of the raceway. *Isn't anybody going to say anything? Are they really going to let him race?*

He glanced back at Gordy, then to his mother and back to Gordy. His mother looked sympathetic, and Gordy just shrugged his shoulders. They were cheaters and nobody was going to do anything about it. Peter watched as Germy Jeremy held up his frog in triumph. He had won his race.

"LADIES AND GENTLEMEN," bellowed the announcer once again. "We have a winner. Two winners, as a matter of fact—Jeremy Jacob's fantastic frog, 'Sir Lancelot,' and Peter (what did you say your name was, boy? Oh, well it doesn't really matter now, does it) and his fabulous frog, Frog? Um . . . yes, Frog.

"At this point, I cannot begin to hazard a guess as to who will win this beautiful trophy. But . . . ladies and gentlemen, I think it's about time we find out, don't you?"

The crowd cheered, and began to chant, "Frog, Frog, Frog, Frog."

"To the starting gate, gentlemen."

Jeremy gave Peter a slight shove, whispering "loser," as he set his gigantic frog on the starting line. He nodded for his dad to be his point man while he headed for the finish line.

"Oops, Mr. Jacobs, sir. No help on this one. The frogs must stay put on their own, until their owners call them. You understand, don't you . . . sir?"

"No matter," Mr. Jacobs smiled his usual oily

smile. "He can win just as well with me or without

me." He marched off to watch the race, confident

that the race was already won.

Peter glanced toward his mother, a worried

smile pasted on his lips, as she blew him a kiss for

good luck. Without thinking, Peter reached out and

planted a quick kiss on the top of Alexander's head,

before placing him on the starting line. "For luck,"

he whispered, patting him one more time before

sprinting toward the finish line, this time forgetting

his lame leg. "For luck."

"On your mark . . . . Get set . . . . Go!"

The crowd began to roar as Alexander flew

down the home stretch. But where was Sir Lancelot?

Laughter? Laughter at the greatest frog in the world?

The mighty champion of the universe?

"Come on, you stupid frog," called Jeremy. "What's the matter with you? Get moving."

But "Sir Lancelot" just yawned and began to rub his eye with his gigantic foreleg. Who was this boy, telling *him*, 'Sir Lancelot the Great,' what to do? He didn't know this boy and if the truth were known didn't really even want to.

The gigantic frog turned and began to hop back to his crate. *Hmmm. Dinner would be great right about now. One good race is sufficient, and besides, I'm hungry, and food Is always better than an old race, isn't it?*

CHAPTER ELEVEN

"Ma! We won! We won!"

"I know, Peter. I am so proud of you—both of you." She tousled Peter's hair and gently rubbed Alexander's head. He closed his eyes, and if he would have been a cat, instead of a frog, he would have surely purred. "Well, Peter. Are you ready to go home and celebrate?"

"He can't go home yet, ma'am," Gordy broke in. "The races ain't over yet."

"They ain't, aren't? But I thought—"

"The frog races are done, but the kid races haven't started yet."

"Kid races?" Peter poured a glass of water into a pie tin and put Alexander in it, just to cool off a bit after the big race.

"Wanta race?"

"Ooh, no. I can't run. I've got this bad leg, see, and—"

"I seen you run. You and Frog. You run real good."

"But I always lose. You go ahead. I'd rather watch, anyway." Peter was content with Alexander's win, but deep inside he longed to feel the wind in *his* face, and a medal around *his* neck.

But that was impossible. People would laugh at him, hobbling down the track. No, it was impossible. A dream. An . . . impossible . . . dream.

He sighed.

"Will somebody PLEASE get that frog off the track? With legs like that, I'm liable to have myself a fine dinner."

The crowd roared once again as Peter glanced over to see what was going on. There was Frog . . . on the starting line . . . his back feet kneading the ground, his head down, streamlined and ready to go.

Peter hobbled as quickly as he could to the starting line and grabbed Alexander, holding him close to his chest as Alexander struggled to be freed. "No, Frog. You can't race this time. This race is for kids, not frogs. Besides, he'll eat you if he catches you." Peter shivered with fear for Frog, and hidden longing for himself. The people smiled affectionately at Peter before turning back to the race at hand.

"On your mark . . . get set . . . go!"

As the flag dropped, Alexander squirmed out of Peter's arms, hit the ground, and flew past the starting line and onto the track. "Stop! Come back! He'll eat you!" Peter's lame leg was forgotten, and he ran like the wind, but a hair's breadth behind the tiny would-be competitor.

Concern for Frog's safety overcame any fears of his own as he struggled to catch his best friend . . . before losing him forever to someone else's hungry stomach.

The weeks of training Alexander, had produced a remarkable change in Peter. He was taller, stronger, and determined. Yes, he was determined to save Frog at any cost. He no longer cared if people made fun of him, or laughed at his ungainly gait. He had to catch Frog before it was too late.

But Alexander was not about to be caught, at least until his boy crossed the finish line. Peter, however, was not thinking of the race. His only thought was to save Frog, his very best friend. The other boys seemed unseen as he left them far behind, wondering just who this new kid was and why they hadn't even been aware of his existence.

Peter scooped up the tiny frog, on the run, clutched him once again to his chest, slowed to a stop, and bent over with exhaustion, his free hand on his knee, panted. "Gotcha."

The crowd began to cheer, and Peter searched the racers to see just who *had* won the big race. But everyone was staring at him. Staring and smiling and clapping and cheering. His mother was screaming and jumping into the air and Gordy was turning cartwheels everywhere.

Before you could say, "Peter won," he was surrounded by boys of all ages, pounding him on his back, and inviting him over to play. *Hey, these guys aren't so bad, once you get to know 'em.*

Peter caught Gordy's eye and motioned for him to join them. After all, what good was having a best friend if you couldn't share him? *Them,* he grinned, caressing one tiny froggy head.

CHAPTER TWELVE

Alexander laid his head against Peter's chest and smiled a gentle froggy smile—sighed a *huge* froggy sigh. With tiny froggy fingers he pushed at the medal hanging around Peter's neck. What a great day.

The coveted trophy had been reluctantly left in the care of his mother and Gordy while he, Peter, and his fabulous frog, Frog, returned to Willow Pond. Peter grinned and set Alexander carefully onto the leaf-strewn soil under the old willow tree. "Look, Frog. I'm hangin' yours right here, so everyone can see."

Alexander stood proudly as Peter hung the large gold medal on the lowest willow branch—the one that almost touched the water and could be seen best from any pad in the pond.

"Frog," said Peter. "Now that you're a champion, you need a name fit for a champion. How about 'Alexander the Great' . . . Alex for short. He was a champion too." He swung his arm in a great arch. "Alexander the Greatest! Just like you. Would you like that?"

Alexander could hardly believe his ears. Not only did he and Peter both win their big races, but Peter knew his name . . . . Peter knew his name . . . . At last, he had a name he could be proud of. One that everyone would remember. And his boy had made it all possible.

Alexander took a giant-sized leap, landing square in the middle of the huge lily pad in the center of the pond. In wonder, he began to hop from lily pad to lily pad, not missing a single one.

The frogs of Willow Pond cautiously peeked their tiny heads above the water, and finding that it was their old friend Bumble, began to sing his praises. No longer would he be known as Bumble, for today he had proven his true worth. "Long live Alexander," they croaked. "Long live the King."

Peter fingered his own medal and grinned. He had grown a lot that summer. He had learned to run, and not be ashamed, and he had made new friends, like Gordy and the boys in town, but his very best friend in the whole world was, and would always be, the little frog who had taught him how to live.

"Long live Alexander," he shouted. "Long live the king."

Made in the USA
San Bernardino, CA
13 January 2014